The Itchy-saurus

Rosie Wellesley

wellcome

The dinosaur jungle was packed
with many creatures, but the
biggest of them all was...

Tyrannosaurus Rex.

T Rex liked to roar and stomp and tear
about the place.

He snacked on squishy jungle beasts
and he was always hungry.

But he tried hard to be kind and calm
and when the day was done, he would
doze beneath the puzzle tree and watch
dragonflies fly by.

Until, one day, his skin began to change.

Where he had once been nice and green,
his scales turned red and hot.

Where he had once been smooth and sleek,
he became all dry and crackly.

His arms began to itch.
His legs began to itch.

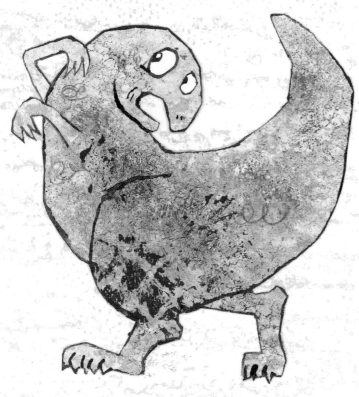

He scratched and scratched but his little arms

just couldn't scratch all over.

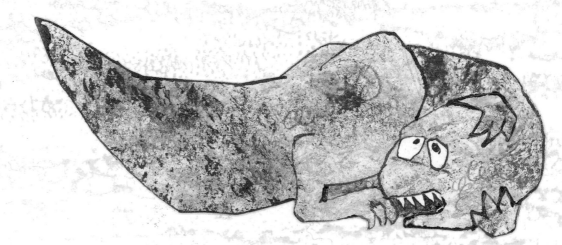

T Rex now was **angry**.

Where he could scratch,
the rash got worse
and where he couldn't,
it drove him *wild*.

ROOOOOAAAR

He chased. He bit.
He forgot ever to be kind.

He became the biggest, crossest, most DANGEROUS dinosaur in the jungle.

RRRR!

One day Doc Bill (the platypus) heard T Rex's fury.

Bill was small and squishy but he was also brave. He liked making healing potions and he knew what he must do.

He must go and find this **angry dinosaur.**

As Bill searched, to give him strength,
he sang his magic potion song:

"Hubble bubble, hubble bubble,

Finally, Bill found T Rex beside the puzzle tree.

He looked most *miserable.*

Bill coughed politely.

"Er… Excuse me…"
he began… but very
quickly stopped when
instead of the expected
snap, T Rex began
to sob.

"*What has happened to me?*" wailed T Rex,

"I cannot sleep, I cannot EAT!
I cannot roar and stomp about.

"Because of this red itchy rash all I
can do is scratch, scratch, scratch.

"I'm no Tyrannosaurus,
I… am… an…

ITCHY-SAURUS!"

"Don't worry, Itchy," said Doc Bill.

"It is just T-Rex-cema.

"I can help but there'll be rules:
1. No biting.
2. **No** stomping
3. **No** scratching!

"And please be patient."

T Rex nodded quietly.

Bill made a cooling bath and set up his cream machine.

He taught Itchy how to weigh and stir and crush and pour, and they sang the magic potion song until the lotion was all done.

"This is very NICE cream," said Bill.

"Very **ice cream?**" asked Itchy, hopefully.

Bill spread the cream all over
Itchy and tucked him up in bed.

For the first time in ages,
the dinosaur slept.

The next day, after more cream,
Itchy waited to feel better.

"I still want to **scratch**," he muttered grumpily.

"You need
distracting,"
said Doc Bill.

So Itchy was taught
to collect wood,
find ingredients
and tend to poorly
jungle creatures.

At bedtime, after cream again, Doc Bill read him
stories about a nice dinosaur who roared and
stomped but was a **vegetarian**.

Itchy started to have fun.

Itchy forgot
to scratch.

After bath and Nice Cream Time Itchy
showed Bill how to roar and stomp.

"No biting!"

reminded Bill.

"Just pretending," muttered Itchy.

Then finally one morning,
T Rex looked down
upon his skin.

It wasn't **red.**
It wasn't **itchy.**

He didn't want to scratch.
He felt his **roar** and
stomp return.

He looked at Doc.
He felt... he felt...

hungry.

He came in close. He **bared his teeth... and...**

"Thank you!" he said.

During the time of the dinosaurs there lived steropodons, ancestors of the duck-billed platypus of today.
There were also dragonflies and monkey puzzle trees.

Although we do not know if dinosaurs had eczema, 20% of children do.
The National Eczema Society is a useful place for more information.

To all children with eczema, especially Tobin.

Special thanks to the patients – children and parents – at the St Andrews Health Centre in Tower Hamlets for your ideas and input into the story. Also to the DIY health team (Clara, Sue and Emma). It could not have been made without you.

**Thanks also to the Wellcome Trust for their funding and patience.
To Jean Robinson from the Royal London Hospital, who has taught me so much about eczema and Mapledene Children's Centre in Hackney, for their help and enthusiasm.**

First published in the United Kingdom in 2018 by
Pavilion Children's Books
43 Great Ormond Street
London
WC1N 3HZ

An imprint of Pavilion Books Company Limited

Publisher and editor: Neil Dunnicliffe
Art director and designer: Lee-May Lim

Layout © Pavilion Children's Books, 2018
Text and illustrations © Rosie Wellesley, 2018

ISBN: 9781843653684

A CIP catalogue record for this book is available from the British Library.

10 9 8 7 6 5 4 3 2 1

Reproduction by Tag Publishing, UK
Printed by Toppan Leefung Printing Ltd, China

This book can be ordered directly from the publisher online at www.pavilionbooks.com, or try your local bookshop.